Love Should Have Brought You Home Last Night

Some people never make it home

(Adults Only)

Stewart Marshall Gulley

This book is a work of fiction. Names, characters, businesses, organizations, places, events and incidents either are the products of the author's imagination or are used fictitiously. Any resemblance to actual persons, living or dead, events, or locals is entirely co-incidental.

No way is this book intended for sexual pleasure, however due to certain situations, the contents and words merely express the true feeling of the sexual thoughts and occurrences that happened during a space of one's life, which makes the book true to life. Its contents are not intended to offend or entice its readers, but to help them to relate to everyday life circumstances.

Copyright 2007

P.O. Box 2063 Los Angeles, Calif. 90078

ISBN: 1-453-649-417

www.stewartmarshallgulley.com

Stemagu7@aol.com

All rights reserved. No part of this publication may be reproduced or transmitted in any form or by any means, electronic or mechanical, including photocopying, recording or any other information storage and retrieval system without the written permission of the author

WARNING!

Prepare for the unknown

Table of Contents

Sunday…………………… Chapter One   6

The Surprise at the Picnic … Chapter Two   41

Shirley at Home …………… Chapter Three   54

Get Me to the Church On Time Chapter Four   69

Prison Can Be Devastating ……Chapter Five   92

Be Careful Who Picks You Up .Chapter Six   118

The Third Floor……………. …Chapter Seven   143

Other Books…………………… ……………   148

Chapter One

Sunday

As usual, the choir stand was packed, because it was first Sunday and we were sure to have an exciting day.

I, Shirley Porter, was there every Sunday along with my bald-headed husband Roger. We have three children visiting relatives in Chicago, but they won't be home for two months. They've already been gone two months, so that will make a total of four months since I've seen my babies. This crazy school system we have now is something else. Whoever heard of children staying out of school for four months? If it were left up to me, they'd stay in school every day for twenty-four hours. That way, Roger and I could have a little playtime, if you know what I mean. The last time, we played so hard that I ended up pregnant with our third child.

Of course, everyone had on his or her white clothes, because it was Mass Choir Sunday. I sat there in my usual Sunday spot and I looked at my husband. I yelled, "Go ahead; you'd better preach." The church people knew those were my favorite words. I feel that if the first lady isn't the first to support her man, then, some little floozy will come around and support him for her, and I don't mean putting a dollar in the tray, either.

For some reason, I wanted to sit with the congregation this Sunday. Usually, the pastor's wife sits on the pulpit, diagonally from the preacher. They all thought I was strange anyway, as I wasn't used to rituals and procedures. You see, God called my husband to preach; but, I just answered the phone.

There I was with a large, beautiful hat looking absolutely divine.

Anyway, the service was going along just fine. Sister Crimson and her husband, Bishop Lee Crimson, from East St. Louis were sitting with me.

I didn't know who it was, but one of those easy, quiet farts came out and I swear it was not mine. Just then, I saw both of the Crimsons' eyes shift left to right, but that wasn't good enough. Bishop Crimson started fanning, blowing the smell down towards me.

My face was turned up; and, as my frown was getting deeper, that little Daryl Johnston says over the microphone,

"Now, the announcements from Sister Shirley Porter."

I could have put my foot in his butt. I don't know about little Daryl, who wears his pants so tightly, but putting a foot in his little butt probably would excite him and he just might like it. Quickly, I got out of my seat and went to the podium with this ugly frown on my face, due to the smell of the gas I had inhaled.

The crazy part about it was that the congregation had frowns on their faces, too, because of mine. They were so used to my lively getting up and cracking silly jokes that this appearance was bewildering. When I thought about it, I said, "Praise the Lord, and thank you, master."

The people were stirred up. I was about to ruin a whole service because of a fart. A bright idea came to me. I decided I would get my husband Roger to preach one Sunday, entitling the sermon "The Power of a Fart." I can hear him telling the story now. "Oh, a fart is just like sin – it affects everybody."

I can hear that voice getting all tuned up; ready to let them have it. I always knew what topic Roger was going to preach, because I was the one who made up the sermons. It was so easy for me to do, because I worked for an advertising firm and we constantly had to come up with headlines that were catchy. And boy, could I come up with some! It seemed like I could find a striking title for everything I did.

I would ask our customers to write a two-page letter of what they do and what they plan to do. I used the same concept on Roger's sermons. It's like talking about Paul in the bible, referring to what Paul did and what he planned to do. Then, I would just fluff it up with a few fancy titles. For instance, do you remember the story about Daniel in the Lion's Den? I read the story and came up with, "Get Your Ass out of The Den." No, I didn't; I was just joking again, but I did think it would fit. The actual title I came up with was "Lockjaw in the Den." In other words, "Shut your mouth." I always enjoyed doing that.

Finally, the offensive smell passed over and I was able to think more clearly. It seemed like the anointing just lifted. What I'm saying is, "Even a fart will kill an anointing." O.K., I'll stop and get serious; but, I just can't help it. I was born into a family of clowns and I mean real circus clowns. It was nothing to see a cousin of mine in a Barnum & Bailey commercial letting people know that the circus was coming to town.

By now, the service was ready to roll. Roger had shifted into fourth gear, preaching "Ten Hot Little Indians." That story was taken from the ten virgins in the bible where five had their oil and the other five didn't. F i v e had to leave and go get oil, because the bridegroom was coming. Now, I know what parents mean, when they say they had to burn that midnight oil. You know, a lot of things go on around midnight – if you catch my drift.

Roger finally finished his dynamic sermon, which wore me out. I can only imagine what some of the other members were thinking. Each one of the ten little Indians was given a name, along with cousins. Each had his or her own thoughts and plans. I had his sermon down to a science so that we could get out on time, but that damn Roger gave each one of them cousins a problem. Boy was I annoyed. I wanted to hurry home and make my cornbread. I don't think it was Okay for him to take so long. There's nothing like a long-winded preacher. I remember one time a preacher prayed so long that I tip-toed out of church, went to the bathroom and urinated, ran to my car to grab a folder, walked back in the church, and he was still praying. He should have taped the prayer and sold it as a sermon.

When Roger finished, I was fine until he asked the congregation if there was anyone who had a hot testimony. I said to myself, "Hell, we are already half an hour late getting out." All of a sudden, this little floozy walked all the way from the back pew, almost seventy rows. Roger has a very large congregation. That little floozy must have swallowed a snake. The way she was moving down the isle, it was like a slimy, subtle wiggle, I might add. But I'm not going to lie. The bitch was built.

Excuse me. I hope the word "bitch" doesn't offend you. I'm sorry, but I'm just real. I'm just like the philosopher who said, "To thine own self be true." I can't remember his name, because I always get names mixed up and people always laugh at me. As far as I'm concerned, Jesse Jackson could have said it.

I have to admit, I was almost jealous as she was walking down the aisle. I may be forty but, baby, I'm stacked, too. I could not take my eyes off of her, and neither could anyone else. I said to myself when I saw her walking, "I don't want to have to whip this bitch's ass on the first Sunday for trying to flirt with my husband." That's just how I felt. People act as if preachers' wives are not supposed to feel anything. Actually, we are just like any other wives and should not have to suppress our feelings. Damn, they don't know from whence I came. Like I said, "God called Roger and I just answered the phone."

She was looking straight at Roger, and he had the nerve to try and give a cute little smile that I'd never before seen. I was steaming and had to reach under my clothes from the back and undo my bra strap. My nerves started to shatter and I said to myself, "I wish that bald-headed mudderfudder would act like he was going to do something." Then, his last sermon would be titled, "I won't be back no more."

The young lady finally stopped in front of the podium and Roger stepped down. Now I know this mudderfudder wasn't trying to make himself look taller by trying to stand straight up. Anyway, I just kept watching the whole thing. He asked her what she wanted from God. I was trying to read her lips, because the microphone wasn't close enough to her for others to hear. Speaking of lips, that sister's lips look liked she worked for the Waffle House. They were huge; but, like I said, the bitch was built. The young lady said she wanted to be made new. I thought to myself that if she were to mess with my Roger that overnight the bitch would be made new. I'd cut her every way but loose.

I'm sorry about my language, but like I said, "God didn't call me, he called Roger and I just answered the phone."

Roger grabbed her head and was getting ready to pray when, quickly coming from the side, was another woman who looked very concerned. She put up her finger and said, "Pastor Porter, could you pray for me along with her, as she's my niece from Chicago? My older sister passed away a few months ago and this is her daughter." Roger replied,

"Why surely, prayer is always in order." He went on and said a quick prayer for them.

About ten minutes later, the service was over. I hugged and kissed a few people, but I slowly managed my way down to that floozy. I stuck out my hand and said, "God bless you darling, and what is your name again?"

The young lady stood straight up and her bust almost hit me in the chin. I mean those titties were perched out there and that little heifer knew it. I promise you, I could have used them for a podium and had enough room to set down a tray with a pitcher of water, along with the bible.

Roger made his way back down from the pulpit again and the young lady said,

"My name is Rene, Rene Smith."

She was answering me but Roger interrupted us, because he had not gotten her name when she had come down the aisle.

"Rene, I am so glad that you and your aunt came to service with us today."

Her aunt reached out her hand and said,

"I'm her Aunt Barbara Glover."

Roger also greeted Barbara and he went on to say, "My wife and I are going to CoCo's for dinner. Would you two like to come?"

When I heard him say that, I felt sweat rolling down the crack of my ass. I was burning and wondering why was he inviting them to join us. Then again, that's just like Roger; always inviting someone somewhere. I already knew he was going to tell me later, "God laid it on my heart to invite them."

I was going to lay something on his ass if anything crazy happened. I guess he'd forgotten the last time he invited a person we didn't know to dinner. That person clipped his watch right off his arm in the name of Jesus. That lets you know how I feel about inviting folks. The bible says, "Know them that labor among you." Hell, Roger didn't know those two ladies, who could have been working in drag for Al Capone.

I just gritted my teeth and took my pretty little self out to the parking lot, continuing to speak to other members as I walked.

Roger yelled, "Shirley, could you escort Rene and Barbara to the car?"

I wanted to tell him to escort them his own damn self, since he was the one who invited them. Instead, the sweet little pastor's wife said,

"Sure honey. I almost forgot them that fast." They both came walking towards me, but Rene had that little smirk on her face as though she already knew I didn't like her.

They followed me and we stood outside of the car. It was very hot that Sunday, so I opened the car doors to let the heat out. I really just wanted to put Rene in there all by herself, lock her up and watch all of her make-up roll down her face. She had enough on to do every woman in the Miss America Pageant.

Waiting for Roger, we all stood beside the car looking like the Three Stooges. I began looking at my watch and wondering what the hell he was doing. I told Rene and Barbara to wait right there until I came back, and I went flashing from the parking lot back into the sanctuary where I found Roger praying for someone. I thought to myself,

"This doesn't make any sense. That cow didn't want any prayer, only attention from Roger. Looking like she weighed 250 lbs, and that was on her left side."

When Roger extended the invitation to anyone who wanted prayer, it was Sister Henry's opportunity to go. However, that cow had not moved. Now, all of a sudden, she wanted prayer. I'm not jealous of my husband, but the bible says: "Watch and Pray." Don't you think I'm watching while he's praying?

I'm just sorry, but you have to watch these so-called sanctified bitches more than the ones on the streets.

I stood at the back door with my hand on my hip. I really wanted to put it way up to the middle of my waist, giving the look as if to say, "Bring your ass on here." But, I didn't. When Roger opened his eyes, looking straight at the back door, he saw me standing there and I knew he was reading my mind. He smiled at Sister Henry, told her to be blessed and headed towards me. You have to understand that Roger is a very good-looking, bald headed man with a nice physique but not very tall. He actually looks like a model; he always shaved all the hair off his face, giving him that clean, white man's look. I guess that's how he grew up. Furthermore, we have an interracial congregation. I think about half the congregation has jungle fever.

Roger apologized for the delay, as usual; and, we went quickly towards the car. Most of the congregation had left and my eyes focused in the direction of our long, black Lincoln Continental. Standing with the doors still open were Rene and Barbara looking like two Bon Bons. Roger was so apologetic to them, it almost made me sick. He had this smile that would send you under, even if you were mad at him. There were times I just wanted to cuss him out, but he would give me this sweet voice. A smile would come over his face that made me want to kill him, because I knew I was about to melt in his arms and forgive him for whatever happened. I have to admit, he always meant well. We were getting into the car and that floozy Rene had the gall to sit in the front seat with Roger. She looked back to see if Barbara and I were going to sit in the back seat. Roger's eyes flew directly to me, because he knew the eruption that was about to come out of me.

"Rene, could you please sit in the back and let my wife of fifteen years sit in her favorite seat up front?" Barbara laughed, because she knew Rene was out of place. I would have just told her straight out, "Get yo' ass in the back", but I have to remember I'm the pastor's wife. I was really ready to take my white hat off and commence to whip her ass, because she had the nerve to act like she didn't want to sit in the back. Rene slowly dragged herself out of the front seat, stood up; and, with this quirky swirl of her head, went to the back door. In my heart, I wanted to trip her, of course. Thank God that gesture did not spontaneously come from my feet.

We all took our proper places and off to CoCo's we went. Rene asked a question and it took all I had to keep from bending over and laughing. As we pulled up to CoCo's, she said, "So this is *Coo Coo's*?" I thought to myself that a Coo Coo House would fit her perfectly." Roger politely said, "It's called CoCo's." Even Barbara was tickled. I knew by that statement that either she had never gone to CoCo's or she couldn't read.

Roger finally pulled into the driveway and, went down a few aisles, looking for a parking space. There just so happened to be a spot right near the front door. Thank God, we didn't have to walk far. Although I was looking good, these pumps I had on were choking the hell out of my feet. I paid two hundred and fifty dollars for pain. Now tell me who's crazy?

Roger parked and we all bailed out of the car. I guess I still had my attitude and making it worse was my snagging my lace dress on the inside lock of the car as I got out. Before I could catch myself, I said, "Damn it." I already knew what was going through Rene's and Barbara's minds, as they heard the pastor's wife use a curse word. To top it off, I saw Rene, with a smile on her face; turn her head, as though she were glad.

Roger quickly asked, "What's wrong?"

I told him that everything was OK. It was just a small snag on my three hundred and eighty-five dollar dress. I knew then that the rest of the afternoon was going to be funky.

For a few minutes, no one said anything else, thinking it would be better to say nothing. Since I had slipped and said a curse word, they did not know what other words I had in store for them if they said something about it. I was cursing before Roger met me, so it wasn't a surprise to him and I didn't care what others thought. Although, when we first met, he hadn't been called to preach.

One morning, he woke up with this preaching revelation and I have been cursing more every since. I have been known throughout the state as the cursing pastor's wife. Many people knew I didn't have that "holier than thou" attitude, because I knew what everyone else was doing, in the name of Jesus. Either I got it through the grapevine or would click my dynamic gift of discernment or intuition. I have to admit that I was pretty good at it; because, when it came to pinning the tail on the donkey, I was always able to stick it where it belonged. I just couldn't figure out why people didn't mind their own business. God already knows what everyone is doing; so why do they need to repeat it or lie about it?

We were all in CoCo's and had been waiting about fifteen minutes to be seated. Rene' had gone to the restroom, leaving the three of us chatting as we patiently waited for our name to be called.

Since Rene was still gone when the waitress came she escorted us to our seats, way across the room, I was hoping that silly bitch would have thought we had left her and gone home. We sat there looking at our menus; and, as I looked up, strolling across the room looking like a cobra came Rene. She looked like she had put on more make-up. I could have sold her face for a voodoo mask.

Barbara noticed Rene's looking for us, but I was not going to budge. Finally, Barbara stood up and waved her hand to make Rene aware of where we were seated. I said to myself, "Damn." The waving of Barbara's hand was fine, but that wasn't what got to me. Rene' saw Barbara and loudly yelled across the room, "Hey, there y'all is!" Everyone in the restaurant looked at her and some began to laugh. I was so embarrassed that I could have turned into a water glass, as though I were not there.

Anyway, she made it to the table and sat down. As she smiled you saw where her lipstick had gotten on her teeth. No one, including me, said anything about it. Because the lipstick was dark, she sat there looking as if several teeth were missing. If I had opened my mouth to say what was on my mind, I'm sure we'd all have had to leave.

As usual, I pretended to be the sweet pastor's wife who thought it proper to keep her mouth shut, although, sometimes, things would just slip and I would get tired of the phony act. My attitude was to make sure I told you up front, so that things would not stick out behind. That way, everyone knew where I stood. That's just who I was. People who run around trying to be someone else and then you talk to *that* person and they're trying to be someone else, too. It was nothing but a bunch of bull.

As far as my little curse blurps were concerned, for some reason, they were always on time and never out of place. People knew I did not play. I was "as crazy as a Betsy Bug", my mother would say. Sometimes, things would come out so fast that I didn't know I had said them. I did not see anywhere in the bible that it said, "Thou shalt not curse." For the uppity church folks, I would try to refrain from cursing. However, some Sundays they would really test my will.

I can remember when Roger and I went to a big church convention in Pittsburgh, Pennsylvania, attended by over fifteen thousand people. Roger was the special guest and we sat on the main stage. A pastor from one of those mega churches in the South got up, asking people to give two thousand dollars a piece. Oh, how he worked that group of people. He used every strategy from parables, sympathy, empathy and faith, to the woman who gave her last penny in the bible. As he spoke, he looked at the ministers on stage; and, by the look in his eye, I knew it was show time.

The way he worded things, if you didn't understand what he was doing, you'd feel cheap, guilty, embarrassed or that God was going to punish you for not giving before you got back to your city. As I sat there beside Roger, I thought that if he got up and gave two thousand dollars, I was going to kick his ass all the way back to St. Louis and would dare him to holler. He knew we did not have that kind of money to give and, also, how I felt about people making others feel guilty. The bible said to give secretly. Those who showed off by giving their money already received their reward – in praise from the audience.

Although we had a large congregation, we were very frugal with our money and sometimes things got pretty tight. All of our bills were now due and we had already squeezed funds to go to the convention. Well, the minister taking the offering kept gnawing at the people. It was a real turn off to me. We had already paid one hundred and fifty dollars each, just for registration. And to this day I still don't know what the hell we were registering.

The minister kept using enticing words and Roger shifted in his seat, as though he was trying to get up. My hand flew down to my right side and I pinched Roger on his butt as if to say, "You had better not move." Would you believe he pulled away from me and stood in that line? Suddenly, I felt gas bubbling in my stomach.

My eyelids started to flutter so quickly that had you stood in front of me, you would have thought there was a fan coming from my face. All I could see were our lights being turned off, car note due and credit card payment being late. We both made good money. Like many people who incorrectly thought they were being frugal, the next thing they knew they had over-extended themselves with pride. Looking at Roger in that line, I started breathing so hard you would have thought I had asthma. What broke the ice was that this minister did not know me from Adam. I guess he thought that my being the pastor's wife, I could pray. Would you believe he called me up in front of all of these people to ask the blessing? I was half spell-bound and the other half was upset with Roger. How was I going to bridle my tongue?

I got out of my seat and looked directly at Roger. He held his head down as though he knew he had to go in deep prayer, because he knew how my mouth was and how I felt about some of these stupid offerings. I went to the microphone; and, just as I got a few words out I said, "Y'all, about some of the du...."

The sound system had gone totally dead. Therefore, no one heard my prayer, not even the minister on stage. Had they heard it, I'm sure Roger would have been banned from the organization. Of course, I would not have minded; because, all I saw were meetings, money and a lot of wasted time. Yes, I was wrong and I did curse over the microphone. Some people probably thought I was talking in tongues, but I was cursing like a sailor and they were shouting hallelujah. I said,

"Y'all are some dumb ass folks. For God to have given y'all wisdom, why are you falling into the con-hype? Pay your tithes and keep on stepping."

As far as offering is concerned, you can give a dollar. Some of these people think they are going to be blessed because they gave two-thousand dollars. Some have not given all year. I know you are supposed to give, but I know what goes on behind these doors. I don't believe in all of those Women's Days and Men's Days and all of these assessments. For some churches, you have to have a second job just to attend.

Anyway, my dear Roger gave the money and just like my inner voices told me when we got home to St. Louis from our trip; Roger had to borrow money from his mother to pay our bills. She always told him, "Boy, you will never be able to keep any money." Roger knew if it wasn't for me, half the time we wouldn't be able to have the good times we did have. That is because, most of the times, I kept to a tight budget; or, at least, I tried to until Roger would do crazy things I didn't know about it.

The only flaw with the budget was that both of our names were on the checking account. Therefore, when Roger would do something stupid, he wouldn't write it down and I would have to cover for him. Those days are past and gone, most of them anyway. I found out it takes time to learn one another and you have a hard enough time trying to learn yourself.

Anyhow, I'm sitting at this table in Coco's looking at Rene, who looks like the make-up artist for the Barnum and Bailey Circus has just done her face. When the waitress brought us the menu, as a joke, she said, "Bon Appetit." Wouldn't you know, that silly Rene answered her and said, "I have an appetite too?" We all looked at one another just waiting to see what she would say next.

Roger told Rene and Barbara to order what they wanted; and, of course, he would take care of the tab. As Rene was looking at the menu, she kept pulling her hands through her imaginary hair, which was twenty inches of cheap synthetic hair. I ordered, then Barbara ordered and now it was Rene's turn. I could have died laughing when she said,

"I want one of *dees intrees.*"

The surprised waitress glanced over at Rene. I mean the smile on her face could easily have fit Bozo the clown. Quickly, the waitress's eyes followed Rene's finger that pointed to entrees.

Rene looked up, because she felt she had pronounced it wrong, with a little snicker coming from me. "Yes, dis one here," she went on, in spite of what the others were smiling at. Then, I almost hit the ceiling when that cow ordered the highest-priced thing on the menu. Roger looked at me as if to say, "Don't you dare open that mouth." Once again, I kept my mouth shut, but on the inside I was calling her all kinds of bitches.

After a while, we all had finished our meals; and, just as I was wiping my mouth, Rene waved to the waitress to come over. Now, I could only think about that movie called *Throw Mama from the Train.* Since we were all ready to go, what in the world could she want now? I was going to find out with all the rest of the stooges. "Could you bring me another slice of apple pie ala *mood*? And put the '*ahs*' cream in a plastic cup," Rene demanded as she licked her fingers. Then, she yelled to the waitress, "I want it to go!"

I knew at that point there was a God and angels, too; because, God told the angels to hold down my arms. Otherwise, I would have slapped the hot-water pee out of her. I kept saying to myself, "Lawd, help me quick. Jesus, you can do a quick thing. I can feel your help coming on. Hold my arms, Lawd." It seemed like magic, when suddenly something came over me and I knew God had sent his angels. I know those angels called me all kinds of names, but they had to do what the Lord told them.

I sat there patiently, while Roger and Barbara lowered their heads down; because, they were so embarrassed. Roger thought he would strike up a conversation to sort of throw things off, so he asked Rene, "What sort of work do you do?"

"I work at a 24-hour *fidness* center," she said as she lifted her breasts. As I have said for the hundredth time, the bitch was built. You can tell she was athletic. So, I just asked her did she work there 24 hours. They all laughed at the table, as well as a few people at the table near us who happened to overhear the conversation. They were laughing harder than we were.

"No I don't, I'm only there three days a week for five hours each day. I also work as a personal coach."

Roger's eyes flickered and he said, "Maybe you can help me." I stomped his toe underneath the table, and I made sure I hit the bad one. It took all he had from saying, "ouch!"

Rene smiled and cooed, "I would love that; it is a co-ed gym, you know."

Just in the nick of time, the waitress came back with the apple pie. Roger handed her his credit card and we waited until she returned. She brought the card right back, Roger signed the charge slip, and she thanked us and left.

We all got up from the table and the pie container was slightly opened. Rene, who was trying to be so cute, somehow managed to tilt the pie and it slid out of the container and onto her. She bellowed,

"Lord!"

I glanced at that heifer and muttered,

"You need to call somebody you know, because it's not the Lord."

It slipped out of my mouth just that fast. Rene scrunched her eyes at me and Barbara turned up her nose. Of course, at that point, I didn't care.

The waitress heard the noise, ran back over, apologized and got her another piece of pie. However, that was not good enough for Rene. Then she asked the waitress who was going to send her dress to the cleaners. The waitress stood there with her mouth wide open and speechless. Roger immediately interceded and said,

"Don't worry; I'll take care of that."

Roger left that nice waitress a ten-dollar tip on the table and we all got up and left. Just as we got to the front door, Rene said she forgot something and went back to the table. Everyone kept walking, but I walked slowly. Out of the corner of my eye I saw that cow pick up the ten dollar tip and put it in her bosom. I just acted as though I did not see anything. The particular waitress that waited on us knew Roger always left a good tip, so I guess she was shocked when she didn't find anything on our table.

I waited until everyone got in the car and then I turned to Roger and said,

"I'm sorry honey, I have to run back to the restroom."

He nodded his head as if to say, "Suit yourself." I got back out of the car, picked up my purse and

went to the restroom. It was the only way that I could

go back into the restaurant and give our favorite

waitress the tip she deserved.

I found her, gave her ten dollars and told her we were having so much fun that we almost forgot to leave it. Had she noticed our table, she would have known I was lying; because, we had sat there hardly saying anything to each other. I made it back to the car; and very lady-like I might add, I gracefully opened the door and sat down.

Roger, in his joking manner inquired, "Did everything come out alright?"

"Like a charm," I chuckled.

Everything was quiet on the way back to the church. We pulled into the parking lot and drove up to an old Mustang. It really would have been a beautiful antique if someone given it a nice paint job, but the body on it was fine. We let them out; and just as we were about to pull away, Roger said to Barbara, "By the way, the church picnic is this Saturday and I would like for you two to come." I felt pee squirting down my leg. I needed a baby wipe, because that statement hit one of my pee nerves. Hey, I have all kinds of nerves, poop nerves, burpin' nerves. You name it and I've got the nerve for it.

Both of them started grinning like Cheshire cats. Then, Roger told them that the directions were in the church bulletin. We finally got away from them, but I didn't tell Roger that Rene picked up the tip. I thought I would keep this episode for safe keeping. When I needed it, I'd blow it on him.

Chapter Two

The Surprise at the Picnic

The week had gone by quickly. I picked out a cute yellow culotte skirt set to wear with my new straw hat. I really loved this particular hat. You'd never see another one like it, because I got the only one on the rack. The hat band was multi-colored with yellow flowers. Roger and I had gotten a late start that morning, because I had been a little horny. Roger always knew what to do when I was persistent about having my needs met. I know the church has its needs, but I have mine, too. From what I can remember, I was here before the church. Now, put that in your kitty and purr.

After we finished our private little church service, I got up and showered again. I intended to have a beautiful day. As the old saying goes,

"A little dab will do ya."

We finally made it to the park, which was loaded with people from our congregation. The men were at the grill and the ladies were dressing the tables. Everyone was laughing and having a ball. It was sunny, but not too hot and a nice breeze would blow by every now and then.

I had also driven my car, as we needed both cars to carry all the food and chairs we needed to bring.

We had been there already about two hours, and the picnic was to be over around four o'clock. They had figured that after cleaning up the area, we would be done about five o'clock. Everything was going fine until about three o'clock, when the booger bear arrived in some yellow hot pants and top with spaghetti straps. Barbara was right beside her. One look at Rene and I screamed to myself, "That bitch has got on my hat. Oh my God, I'll never live this down." I broke out in hives and passed gas at the same time.

Talk about a coincidence! I was furious, but I knew I had to think fast. I slowly eased back to my car without anyone's paying close attention to where I might be going. Luckily, I remembered that I had a sheer yellow scarf in the trunk of my car; so. I pulled off the multi-colored scarf on my hat and replaced it

with the sheer yellow one. I took out a small pair of scissors I had in my purse and I cut half the top off of my hat and fluffed my hair out of the center. I probably looked like a rooster but I was different and still cute. I would not be at ease looking at her with the same hat and scarf as mine. Of course, I later found out that there
were two hats left on the rack. That cow bought the other one and I guess that left the last one for me.

I made it back to the park area; and fortunately, it seemed no one noticed that I had left, nor did anyone say anything about the scarf I had replaced or my hair coming out of the top of my hat. You know how we women are; we fuss about how some men don't like us. In reality, we don't like each other that much either. In a matter of minutes, the picnic would be over, so why had those two come this late? I do not know. Both of them went straight to the tables where all of the good eating was, and those two were grabbing food like they hadn't been fed in years. I just watched their hog- eating performance along with a few others.

Not one word came out of my mouth. Like a tree planted by the river, I would not be moved. It came out in one of the conversations I later overheard that Rene lived by herself and so did her aunt. I could only imagine what went on at Rene's apartment. Quickly, I decided to push that thought out of my mind and think about something positive and beautiful. I was sitting about two picnic tables away from Rene and Barbara and they both waved and smiled, but neither came over to my table. I said to myself, "Those old scummy-looking cows don't fool me."

Roger was all over the place. Rene had gotten a large cup of ice and poured fresh lemonade into it. Very daintily, she got a straw and slid it slowly inside the cup as though she wanted someone to see all of her movements. What got me was when she put her big lips on the straw. Roger just so happened to be passing by; and Rene with this sweet look on her face, she slowly began to suck from the straw as she looked at Roger. I was watching the whole damn thing and I was just waiting for my chance to hear the wrong thing come out of either one of their mouths. I should have worked for the FBI because of how well I could read lips. Those big lips of Rene's were like reading a billboard. Uh, Oh! Here it comes.

"Hello Pastor Porter, how are you?" inquired Rene slowly.

"Oh, just fine. Trying to greet everyone and making sure everybody is having a good time."

"Take your time, pastor; you don't want to overlook an opportunity, if you know what I mean."

I read the lips and I hopped off the bench to fly over there and snatch that hussy; but, I tripped over one of the legs on the picnic table and twisted my ankle. Roger flew over to help me, and one of the ladies nearby ran and looked inside one of the coolers to scoop up some ice for an ice pack. She hurriedly poured the ice in a plastic bag and came toward me.

Roger wanted to take me to the hospital, but I told him that I would be fine. Thankfully, I really didn't hurt my ankle as badly as everyone thought. However, I yelled so loudly that you'd have thought Jesus had fallen. Strangely, I didn't say one curse word when I fell. I guess my response was really full of pain more than anger. I sensed what was going on and I was hot and angry!

I sat there like bubbling brown sugar, while lots of people walked over and showed concerned about my ankle.

At this point, I looked up; and, straight in front of me was Rene, still sucking on that straw like a Hoover Vacuum Cleaner. She knew I was looking and she slowly turned her head. If my vision was correct, I saw her rolling her eyes. Surprisingly, I was behaving like Mary in the bible; I just pondered things in my heart. However, I'm sure Mary was not pondering what I was thinking about doing to Rene.

It started to get very late and the people began cleaning up and preparing to leave. Deacon Jones escorted me to the car and I told Roger that Deacon Jones was going to drive me home in my car. Roger gave me a kiss and we left.

I had gone home, but being a thinking woman, I thought I had better seriously keep my eyes on Rene and ask a few friends to watch her. Recalling that a storm was on the way, Roger went back to the tables and hurried the people along. Thank God they had all finished having fun at the picnic. Roger headed for his car.

Rene and Barbara were almost the last to leave. It had not really dawned on Roger that they were still in the parking lot, sitting in Barbara's car, which was parked beside Roger's. Rene got out of the car and lifted up the hood. As she lifted the hood, she made sure her butt was sticking way out for Roger's undivided attention. There was something wrong with the car; so Roger, in his usual manner, went to assist.

The car would not start. He went back and forth, while Rene's worked the ignition, trying to get it going. He also tried to give it a jump start, but nothing happened. Roger said to her,

"Is there something else I can do?"

Rene positioned her lips in the most sensual way she could and said,

"Yes, I believe there is. Could you take me home?"

Roger fell right into the lion's den and told her he would. He did not know that Rene had planned the whole thing, by going under the hood earlier and cutting one of the wires so the car would not start. He really didn't think clearly, because her aunt was there and she could have easily taken Rene home. There's no telling what reason Rene gave him to justify her aunt's inability to take her. Anyway, the ride home for Rene was settled and the parking lot was cleared.

At this time, the only two ready to leave were Roger and Rene. They both walked to Roger's car and Rene hopped in the passenger's side and Roger in the driver's side. As soon as he sat down, he laid his cell phone down in a little basket that separated the two seats in front.

Although she was sitting down, Rene had not closed the car door. The door was wide opened and she slowly looked down towards her lap as her eyes swiftly moved back and forth if to say, "I'm a lady. Could you please go around and close my door?" Roger had a perplexed look on his face, but he got the picture. He hopped back out and went around to close the door. He thought to himself that he didn't do that for his own wife, so why was he doing it for Rene? As they drove along for several miles, Roger realized he really didn't know where he was going. It was as though he had lost all consciousness. Rene just sat there. He gave a slight little cough and asked,

"Aren't you going to tell me the directions or something?"

Rene was smiling. "Since you didn't ask, I thought you just wanted to go for a little joy ride."

It hit Roger that he may be in a little trouble. Until now, he had not realized that Shirley was at home wondering what was taking him so long. Rene finally spoke up and said,

"Oh, I get these streets all confused. We are headed in the wrong direction. As a matter of fact, my Aunt lives around the corner. Can we stop there?"

Roger knew he didn't have time for all of that, as he was already late getting home.

"Where's my cell phone? I need to call my wife." As he shuffled in the little basket between the seats, he became frantic.

"I didn't see a cell phone, sweetie," said Rene with a sneaky look on her face. Roger shot her a look when she called him sweetie.

"I know I had it; I'm sure I put it in here."

"When we get to my aunt's house, you can call your wife and then we can run back to the park to see if you left it there. Roger knew the storm was coming and he really needed to be at home. Rene persuaded Roger to go to her aunt's house, where he parked on the street without noticing the "no parking" sign. They got out of the car and walked down the long driveway to the side entrance. Rene tapped on the door and Barbara answered,

"What are you doing here?"

"We made the wrong turn to go to my house and Pastor Porter lost his cell phone," she replied.

"Well, come on in and have a seat."

Roger and Rene entered the house. It was tastefully decorated but a little sensual, with shear drapery gathered across the bed post. The living room had shear draperies, as well, extending across the room in different directions. Surprisingly, it had a sort of Pakistanian look, but it was really pretty. The low light behind the chairs and plants created a very sensual atmosphere.

Now, for the ultimate surprise! When Roger asked to use the telephone, Barbara said that it had just got turned off yesterday. She had gotten to the main office after it closed and was unable to pay the bill. Roger knew he had to leave immediately. While Barbara was still talking to Roger, Rene had gone to the kitchen to get a glass of cranberry juice. To Roger, it appeared as though Rene had come from out of nowhere with this mysterious juice.

"Pastor, drink a little juice and slow your butt down and rest yourself for a few minutes. I heard one of your tapes and you said we ought to slow our butt's down so we can think."

That title "Slow Your Butt Down" was one of the titles Shirley had given him for a sermon pertaining to the scripture don't be anxious for nothing (Phil.4:6). Roger chuckled because that was definitely the title of one of his sermons. He sat down and began to sip the juice. As he was sipping, there were many things going on in Rene's mind as she watched Roger get very sleepy. The night was filled with mystery, for Roger had fallen into the hands of someone who was about to destroy his whole life. Roger fell asleep.

Chapter Three

Shirley at Home

The house was in a tizzy. Shirley was walking back and forth. She had no idea where Roger was. The storm had set in and people were warned to stay inside, if possible. Shirley called several members and they all said that there had only been a few people left at the parking lot: a woman with yellow shorts and a straw hat and one with white slacks and an orange blouse. There were only two people these could have been: Rahab and Esther the Queen, better known as Rene and her Aunt Barbara. In Shirley's heart, she knew Roger was with them; but, in the same breath, she felt something could have happened to him.

Shirley was furious, she fell to her knees and began to pray and cry. She, asked God for strength for the worst imaginable thing that could possibly have occurred. She prayed and cried so badly that she fell asleep on the same spot.

The night passed, and when Shirley awakened, it was eight o'clock Sunday morning. This also meant there would be a lot of questions from people asking where the pastor was.

Shirley had no choice but to call the police. It is ironic that when she called, they already knew where his car was. It had been towed the previous evening for being illegally parked in front of Barbara's house. Instead of parking in the long driveway, he chose the street. On the phone, Shirley told the police that the pastor was missing. From his license plates alone, the police department already knew whose car it was, since Roger was prominent in the community. A new officer, not yet familiar with Roger's status, had the car towed. Otherwise, he would have tapped on the door. Thank God, he didn't. Shirley was given the address where the car had been found. The police officer also asked her if she needed him to go with her.

Shirley replied, "Hell, no. God has got my back."

After slipping on some clothes and with a very slight limp, she flew out the door. The ground was still wet. Shirley looked at the address again. She had written it on a large, pink sheet of paper and laid it on the car seat beside her. She nervously started her car and took off for 3426 128th Street. Before she had much time to think, she was in front of the house, which was two doors from the corner.

Her heart began to beat rapidly as she approached the door to knock. Stepping back from the door she noticed a side window that was at eye-level. She peeked in the window and squinted, her mouth dropping. There, lying asleep on the floor, with no shirt or pants on, was her dearly beloved Roger. Shirley froze in place as though life had thrown her a solid punch. Seeing Roger on the floor was not the ultimate, for over in the corner was Rene, brushing her fake hair and smiling. Her aunt was stretched out, asleep on the sofa wearing just a bra and butt-naked. It was the nappiest pubic hair Shirley had ever seen. All she could say was, "Oh, my God, all of those raisinets." Shirley turned her head, not realizing she was really in a state of shock. She thought of herself as a strong woman who was meeting the biggest challenge of her fifteen years of marriage.

Shirley walked slowly to her car with a look on her face as if to say, "Its time to leave earth and die, and this would be the best time ever." For all of these years, she had been faithful and, yes, also a bitch. Still, she was true to her man. It was as if her whole world had been invaded and nothing mattered. As she was walking away from the window, she dropped the pink piece of paper with Barbara's address on it. It was a fancy piece of paper addressed to Mr. & Mrs. Roger Porter. It had flowers around the edge, which came from a promotional company having a reception and inviting Roger and Shirley to attend. It was from one of Shirley's advertising clients. The wind blew the pink paper and it got stuck in some small hedges by the door.

With her head down, Shirley walked slowly to the car, opened the door and just sat there. She was too hurt to cry and too angry to do anything but start the car and made a quick U-turn from her parking spot.

She went to the police station and reported that Roger was doing fine, but she didn't give any details of how she found him. She even paid for the car's being towed and let them know that someone would be down later to pick up the car and bring it home. The officer looked at her as though he already knew what could have happened.

He had a great idea what she could have found at 3426 128th St.

She quickly paid the fee, and told the officer to keep the change. How often does anyone tell someone associated with the courts to keep the change? She made it home by ten o'clock, but there was no Roger. She then called Rev. Lewis, the assistant pastor, and asked him to preach the morning service because Roger wasn't feeling well. Rev. Lewis tried to ask Shirley a lot of questions; but, by the tone of her voice, he knew there was something wrong. Although he asked her if everything was OK and she said "yes", he could read between lines, realizing there was something else. However, he let it go.

    Shirley went to church and did not sit in her favorite chair. A million things were going through her mind. "How could Roger do this to me?" A tear slowly rolled down her cheek, but she wiped it immediately. She was fighting to contain her true feelings, for the real pain inside was unbearable.

About five o'clock that evening, Ronnie, a young man from the church, brought Roger's car home. Shirley gave him forty dollars for his troubles. He didn't want to take it, but she insisted. He thanked her and then a bright idea came to Shirley. She had Ronnie jump back in Roger's car and follow her in her car back to Barbara's place. Ronnie didn't know what it was all about; and, seeing his worried face, Shirley said to him,

"Don't worry darling. I will make this worth your time."

Ronnie followed her, as instructed. He got on his cell phone, called a buddy and said,

"Man, I don't know what's going on, but I believe something heavy is getting ready to go down at the church. I've got to go, but I'll beep you back."

They drove to 3426 128th St. Shirley slowed down and Ronnie pulled up beside her. She told him to very slowly pull the car into the driveway, turn off the engine and hop into her car with her. Once again Ronnie said to himself, "This is some freaky deal."

Had he said it out loud, Shirley would have agreed. Ronnie did as told and then went to Shirley's car. The way he was shuffling almost made Shirley burst out laughing, because Ronnie weighed three hundred and sixty pounds and watching him tip-toe across the grass was something comical to see.

Ronnie got in to the car and off they went. Shirley thought she would play the game so that Roger would have no excuse not to get home. Of course, he would not have known the car had been towed and returned.

After dropping Ronnie off, Shirley made it safely back home. Shirley went into their beautiful home, looked around and went to the kitchen. In the far right corner, bottom left is where she kept her wine. She pulled out a large bottle, uncorked it and filled it to the rim of the biggest goblet they had. She went to the upper cabinet and pulled out a box of Ritz Crackers. Picking up her wine, she went to the dining room table and tipped the goblet up. She ate a few crackers, threw her head back and said,

"Communion was just great."

Shirley sat a while, got her thoughts together and slowly pulled herself up from the table. She went into the kitchen, turned out the light and headed for the bedroom. It was about 8:30 in the evening. All of a sudden, she heard a car skid in the driveway. Sure enough, it was Roger, in a panic. He hopped out of the car and ran into the house, grabbing Shirley. All he could say was,

"Honey, I'm sorry I'm late."

At this point it was going to take God and seven responsible people to keep her from beating Roger's ass. Then she thought, "He's trying to play stupid like he has amnesia."

Shirley, with droopy eyes from drinking, replied,

"Well, what took you so long to get here. Did they widen the park while you were there."

He answered, "I got tied up with a few members. Did you pull me out something to wear for church in the morning?"

Shirley looked at him and jokingly said, "Why not the tan suit?"

"Oh sure, that will be fine," he whispered.

After what she had seen through Barbara's window, Shirley was waiting for an explanation of where he had been for over 24 hours. Shirley began to talk to God; and for some reason, she felt that she couldn't get an answer. The reality was she couldn't forget Roger's lying on the floor with no shirt on, Barbara with no panties and Rene smiling in the mirror, wearing a nightgown. She just couldn't shake the memory. Roger sensed she had an attitude; but, after fifteen years of marriage, he had gotten used to her moods and didn't say anything.

In this case, however, was Shirley's attitude was more serious than he thought. Shirley never opened her mouth regarding what she saw. She laid out Roger's tan suit for the next morning, which would be Monday and not Sunday like Roger thought. Shirley played the whole scenario until she got in the bed and Roger threw his leg across hers, as though he was urging for some sex. Shirley tried to knock his leg clean across the room.

Roger jumped and asked, "What's wrong with you?"

She rolled over to her side of the bed and flipped the cover over her head. Roger sat straight up and thought about how Shirley acted when she's pissed. He just slowly eased back down and pulled the covers up to his neck, carefully shifting his eyes in her direction.

As Shirley lay there, wondering how she was going to handle this, she began to squirm and bite the end of her pillowcase. This was very annoying to Roger, who reached over to the lamp on the nightstand and turned it on. Because there was only one lamp in the room, he had to reach over Shirley to do this. Shirley elbowed him in his chest, almost knocking the wind out of him. He flipped over, grabbed his chest, stood straight up and yelled,

"What the hell is wrong with you. What kind of love is this?"

Shirley rolled her eyes; and with a look that could kill, she replied,

"Kind of love you say? What do you know about love? Love should have brought your ass home last night."

Roger was speechless. "What are you talking about?" he yelled.

"Don't you play dumb with me, *preacher man*! What kind of fool do you think I am?" screamed Shirley.

Roger had never before seen Shirley so furious. He then responded, "What you mean, love should have brought me home last night?"

Shirley hopped up and began to pace the floor, "Save the drama for your mama."

She picked up the alarm clock and threw it at Roger, who swiftly ducked. Back and forth, they argued. Shirley had a million curse words to introduce to the four walls in the room. They were both in a rage. However, Roger didn't know why they were fighting. At the top of her voice, Shirley finally told it all to him, as the neighbors listened.

"You couldn't wait to get to that little stinking bitch Rene, could you?"

Roger, with his eyes bugged out, responded, "What do you mean? I haven't been with that bitch, I mean that young lady."

Shirley had gotten to Roger and now he began to curse. Shirley continued,

"I know where you were, preacher man."

The argument went on and on until they were both exhausted. Shirley snatched a blanket off the bed and went into the living room to finish her sleep on the sofa. Roger lay in the bed and before he knew it, he had fallen asleep.

The early morning sunlight hit Roger in his eyes. He immediately hopped up to prepare himself for Sunday morning service while Shirley slept on the sofa. He peeked in the room to see if she had gotten up; but, because she had called her company early and left a message that she wouldn't be in, she didn't budge.

Roger thought he should say something, although he was very hesitant to say anything for fear of starting another argument that would turn into another long session. He turned to Shirley and said,

"Are you going to church?"

Shirley just laid there. Roger asked again,

"Are you going to church?"

Of course, she had heard him the first time and before you knew it, she yelled,

"Mudderfudder, when did you start going to church on Monday morning?"

Roger shook his head twice and then he said to himself, "This woman is dreaming and has lost her mind. She doesn't even know what day it is."

He knew she still had an attitude and she probably was jealous of Rene. He felt she was just conjuring up something. Roger hurriedly hopped in the shower and freshened up. The room was in a mess, but still hanging on the door was his tan suit. He grabbed the suit, got his tie and shirt and put them on quickly. Then, he was out the door on his way to preach to no one.

Chapter Four

Get Me to the Church On Time

He hopped in the car and turned on his favorite gospel station, but because it was Monday morning, the music was R& B. Roger thought the dials had gotten switched. He backed out of the driveway and saw that most of the cars in the neighborhood were gone. Usually on Sunday morning there were a lot of people home.

He kept on driving and saw groups of children getting off a big yellow school bus. Roger knew then that something was wrong; and looking down the street and seeing a Seven Eleven store, he pulled in. He got out of his car, walked in, went to the counter and poured himself some coffee.

As he added the cream and sugar, he kept looking around. He decided to ask the young lady beside him a question.

"Could you tell me what today is?"

Just before she was ready to answer, one of his members spotted him and yelled,

"Hey Rev. Porter, we missed you yesterday, but, Rev. Lewis still did a fine job."

Roger could only smile and say, "God bless you."

As the member hurried out the door, the young lady to whom he had asked the question, tapped him on the shoulder and said,

"Sir, it's Monday, just in case you still wanted to know."

"Thank you very much," he said in a very slow and quiet voice, while looking out the window, watching the many cars going by. Roger paid for an expensive cup of coffee because prices had changed. However, he was in such shock he didn't pay any attention and went to his car. He sat in the parking lot for quite a while and could not move. The only thing he could say to himself was, "Where have I been?" He didn't know that the worse was yet to come.

Roger drove back home and pulled into the driveway. He was very hesitant to get out of the car, not knowing what Shirley was doing on the other side of the door. He stared at it as though he were in space. He got out of the car, closed the door and went to the side entrance. When he stuck his key in the door, it did not fit. He tried all of his keys and none of them seemed to fit either of the doors. He walked to the side and banged on the door.

About five minutes later someone came to the door and said,

"Who is it?"

To which Roger replied,

"It's me Roger, and who are you?"

The voice on the other side asked him who he was looking for.

"I live here," yelled Roger.

The lady on the other side said,

"I don't know who you are, but I've lived here for the past twenty years. I believe you have the wrong address, sir."

Roger was stunned. He knew his house. He decided to run next door and knock on old lady Iverson's door. It always took her a long time to come to the door, so he was prepared to wait a few minutes. Strangely enough, the door was immediately opened by a young lady with long, gorgeous hair, very beautiful features but a very bad case of acne on her cheeks. She then said to Roger,

"May I help you."

Roger took a big gulp. "Yes, I'm looking for Mrs. Iverson."

The young lady opened her eyes in astonishment. "You mean you knew her?

Roger's jaws became tight. "What do you mean did I know her, where is she?

The young lady, with sympathetic eyes, told him that Mrs. Iverson died about twenty years ago.

"Who are you," she asked.

"I'm her next door neighbor and I just talked to her yesterday."

"Sir, she began, "I don't know what this is about, but I have to go." As she began to close the door, Roger stuck his hand in the doorway.

Wait, can I ask you one more question?"

"Yes, you can, sir, but please make it quick. I'm running late for work."

Roger began to sweat and asked, "What's today's date?"

Of course, he believed it was May 3, 2006, as the church picnic had been on May 2.

Surprised, she repeated his question, "You want to know the date?"

"Yes, yes,,he gasped.

"Why, it's May 3rd, sir."

Roger yelled, "Oh thank you, thank you, I'm not going crazy."

The bewildered lady then added, "I've never seen anyone that excited about May 3rd and if the year will help you, it's 2026."

Roger's mouth flew open and his whole countenance changed.

"What did you say?"

"I said, it's 2026, sir, and now I have to go."

She immediately closed the door and went to her window, peeking through the blinds to see if Roger had left.

Roger walked back to his car and slowly sat down, once again bewildered. The only thing he knew to do was to go to his church and pray. Roger had a large congregation, but it was an old structure built in the early 1800's and had beautiful stained-glass windows and all the ornate trimming on the doors. While driving down the street, his mind was darting all over the place, as he stared at the newly-modeled cars. and the new businesses in the neighborhood.

He made a sharp, left turn onto Stanley Blvd, the street on which his church was located. His mouth flew wide open; because, on the very corner where his church should have been, there was a new

100-unit apartment complex. He held his head on the steering wheel and allowed his tears to flow. Finally, he decided to get out of the car and walk to the front door of the complex.

It was a security building and you had to dial the unit number to gain access to the building. While he was at the door looking at all the names posted, a young lady was coming out, so he hurriedly entered through the door before it closed. He stood in the beautiful lobby in amazement at how lovely it was. There was a nice waiting area beside the elevators and he decided to take a seat. There he was, sitting in St. Louis, Missouri, all confused. In front of him were some old magazines and he was attracted to one that read "*The History of St. Louis.*"

Picking up the magazine and flipping through the pages, he gasped when he saw a detailed picture of his church. The accompanying article explained that there had been an uproar about the demolition of the church. However, the city won the battle and a new 100-unit apartment building was constructed.

The woman who started the protest to save the building would receive one of the units free of charge. Her name was Shirley Porter. Roger froze for a moment; and when he snapped out of his shock, he returned to the front door to check the names of the tenants. To keep the door from closing, he took off one of his shoes and stuck it in the doorway. He immediately went to the letter "P" and saw "S. Porter". It had to be his Shirley.

It had not dawned on him that he was in this new building looking for his wife whom he had just seen yesterday. It was as though he had flipped into the *now*, but there was still a part of *yesterday* lingering and wanting answers for *today*.

The unit number was 108, which meant she was on the first floor. Roger took his shoe out of the door and went back into the lobby to pull himself together. He knew that if Shirley answered the door, it would only be a hallucination, which he was experiencing. He stood up and walked through the steel door leading to all the units on the first floor. After thinking about it, he realized that if he went back to the front door and pushed her button, she would have to answer to let him in the door.

Roger went to the main door, held it open this time with one hand and reached over and pushed the button for #108. The phone rang and was picked up by an answering machine. The voice, which Roger did not recognize, had the sound of a feeble older person. He hung up without leaving a message.

Unbeknownst to Roger, Shirley Porter was at home, crippled, and it took her a long time to come to the phone.

When she picked up the phone, Roger was gone. Roger figured that this Shirley Porter had a connection to him, but he wasn't sure what it was. He decided to leave the building and come back tomorrow.

Roger left and drove off. He had gotten a little hungry and decided he'd stop at Kentucky Fried Chicken. He pulled into the parking lot, sitting another minute, thinking about Shirley. He took out his wallet from the glove compartment and got out of his car, saying to himself, "I think I'll get a regular three-piece dinner."

He entered the building, opening his wallet to pull out a five dollar bill, he looked up at the sign and could not believe his eyes. A three-piece dinner was now $13.85.

"What the hell is going on", he asked in a loud and clear voice.

The cashier put her finger over her lips to get him to lower his voice and then told him that they hadn't changed their prices in 20 years. Where had he been? Furthermore, they did not accept cash, but did he have a chip on the inside of his wrist?

"What chip are you talking about," he asked.

"Sir, we use only the chip system to buy anything. This chip has your social security number as well as your address on it. We must keep track of all purchases in this new economy."

Roger could not believe what he was hearing and he couldn't take anymore of this twenty-year syndrome. He told the cashier he would return.

He went to the restroom and had been in there only five minutes. When he came out, his bottom lip hung down. He was standing outside the bathroom of a nude beach. There was no Kentucky Fried Chicken anywhere. He looked left and right. All he saw were naked bodies.

The burning sun made him thirsty and he spotted a water fountain twenty feet away. As he walked toward it, a naked woman rushed in front of him and bent over to get a drink. All Roger could see was her butt. He turned his head in embarrassment; but, when he turned around, there was a man behind him with an erection, watching the lady who was bent over. Roger felt he was literally between a rock and a hard place. The woman finished drinking, turned and smiled at Roger. Roger went to bend over for a drink, then stood straight up and asked the guy with the erection if he would move back. Roger feared he would get stuck.

Next, Roger bent back over and took a couple of sips and then stepped aside, allowing the man behind him to take a quick drink to "cool off", as the saying goes.

Dazed, Roger began walking, slowly getting used to the place. In the distance, he noticed some very large rocks, with only one or two people on them. Roger thought it looked like a safe place to be alone. He must have passed three hundred bare butts while getting to the rocks. Without feeling any temptation, he made it. He climbed two of the smaller rocks and was then able to scramble up on a rock that was six feet tall.

He sat there, looking across the beach at all of the bodies. Then he began to concentrate on the beautiful, blue water. He had no idea what beach or island he was on, but without the nudity, it was beautiful.

He was getting a little tired and laid back on the rock with his face toward the sun. As he closed his eyes, he heard a voice saying,

"Oh shit, I'm almost there."

Roger himself raised up, looked around and he saw a couple making love between the rocks. He slowly eased down the rock, escaping the drama of making love. For some reason, that sexual episode did not bother Roger as much as it normally would have. He was too busy focusing on where he was and thinking back to when he came out of the restroom at Kentucky Fried Chicken.

Roger was getting hot from the sun and looked pretty strange walking around dressed in a shirt and pants. He thought it couldn't hurt if he took off his shirt and tied it around his waist. Roger was a very good-looking man and had a nice physique. Several women eyed him. One woman passed by him and said,

"Hey good-looking, whatcha got cooking?" He smiled and continued on his way to the beach.

Coming toward him was a very beautiful and fully- clothed young woman. She also saw him from afar. As they approached each other, he noticed there were tears in her eyes. He passed by her; and then thinking maybe she needed some help, he turned around and spoke to her.

"Excuse me young lady, are you alright? I mean, can I help you with something?"

The young woman turned, and with a saddened face, said,

"No I'm OK. I just feel a little lonely. Today is my husband's birthday. He died ten years ago."

Roger thought it strange for this beautiful woman to still be in mourning for a lost husband after ten years.

Across the way, there was a concrete wall about four feet high. He asked her to come over there and sit a minute, thinking maybe he could give her some comforting words. She agreed and told Roger how her husband, who was killed in a plane crash, had left her pregnant. Unfortunately, because of the stress she endured, she had suffered a miscarriage.

After they talked for a long time, she stood up and began walking towards a beautiful, yellow tent on the sand. She invited Roger to go with her.

"Where are you going?

She pointed west.

"That's my tent out there. Every now and then I sleep here at the beach. No one bothers me. Will you come and talk with me there?"

Roger was a little reluctant but he went, since she was as fully-clothed. As they walked, he asked her why she still had her clothes on. She replied that she was a very private person, but she liked the nude beach. Roger didn't understand that answer, but he let it go. They made it to the tent and both went inside. She offered Roger something to drink. It was cranberry juice, again.

Roger said, "Uh, no thank you. Do you have some water?" Roger vaguely remembering what had happened to him the last time he drank cranberry juice, which was offered to him by Rene some time ago.

"Surely," she politely said and reached in her cooler to pull out a quart-size bottle of water.

She kept on talking and, very smoothly, the young woman touched Roger's hands. He did not remove her hand. The sun had gone down and it had gotten dark, many people had left the beach. There were only a few tents scattered here and there.

The young lady removed her hand and very elegantly took her long slim arm and reached across Roger to turn on her CD player. As she reached over, her dress rose ever so slowly up past her thigh, revealing her lack of underwear. Roger swallowed three or four times, while attempting to look in another direction; but, it was as though she had a magnet between her legs, and he could not stop looking.

She slowly sat back up and saw sweat running down Roger's face. Next, she reached into her bag, pulled out a cloth and dabbed Roger's forehead. As she rubbed the cloth across his eyebrows, his eyes closed. She slowly helped him to lie down and he dozed off.

She closed the opening to her tent and reached into her cooler to open a small bottle of wine. It was difficult to remove the cork, but she managed finally. In doing so, she broke one of her candy-apple red fingernails. She poured herself a nice glass of wine, burned some incense and stared at the sleeping Roger.

Then, she put the glass down and reached over to begin rubbing Roger's chest. She massaged it from left to right. Next, she rubbed his shoulder, as she eased slowly over his nipples. Very softly, she kissed his stomach. Slowly, Roger began to respond by making moaning sounds. She loosed his belt and commenced unzipping his pants. Reaching inside, she got a handful of his male genital. "Oh my God," she thought. She pulled out Roger's penis and began pulling on it. He moaned and moaned. She enjoyed pulling on Roger's penis until he had gotten a stiff erection. At that moment his eyes opened and he howled, because he was lying on a hospital table, being prepared to be circumcised - and the doctor was pulling on his penis! Roger shouted, "What in the hell is going on?"

The doctor, a foreigner, said to him,

"Well Mr. Porter, if you would like to cancel the operation you can."

Roger replied, "I'm forty years old and if I had this extra flesh this long, I deserve to keep it."

He immediately hopped off the table, put his shirt and pants on and flew out the door, only to find himself over in India.

Bewildered, he asked himself, "What am I doing in India?" Roger started to run and kept on running. He was in the market area. He was knocking over baskets and stepping over children. He was behaving like a maniac.

The India Police spotted him and chased him. When they caught him, he was handcuffed, driven to a police building and taken to a cell. The first thing they asked him for was his passport. Roger, out of breath, and barely able to talk, loudly asked,

"What passport are you talking about. I'm an American and I don't need a passport?"

The policeman, in a rage, said, "Sir, if you don't have a passport, you will never get out of this country."

Roger began to tussle with the officer, who threw him down, slapped him, back-handed him and spat on him. "When you get your passport, we'll talk," the officer shouted, while slamming the gate to the cell block.

Roger dropped his head between his legs, feeling he had totally lost his mind. After being in the cell about four hours, he was brought for his dinner a flour and water mixture that looked like mush, along with a piece of molded bread. Flies were swarming around the bread as though it were a fly convention. He took the bread and mopped the mush up to eat it with his fingers, as there were no forks or spoons. Later, they brought him a rusty can which was filled with dingy water. Roger was in no condition to be picky, as he wondered where the Sparklett's Water delivery man was. They only allowed him five minutes to eat, then giving his leftover food and drink to the man in the next cell. The smell of urine and feces was horrendous. Roger crawled on the floor back into the corner of his cell and got into a fetal position. He was deeply depressed, as though he was going through a Job experience he had read about in the Bible. He felt like cursing God for all the misery he had been put through, but Roger's lips uttered moans of agony. "This can't be real", he thought, as he watched a small lizard dash across the room. Roger had gone through so much that day that he was afraid to fall asleep for fear of awaking up to somewhere worse.

Just then, he heard the beautiful music of India. Managing to pull himself up and peek through the very narrow window, covered with bars, he saw many women dressed in gorgeous sheer fabrics, dancing in the streets. There had been a new queen appointed, and they were shouting her name. "Queen Shirley, all hail Queen Shirley!" Roger was spellbound and couldn't believe his ears. Putting his index fingers in his ears, he turned round and round. This could not be true.

He began to bang his head against the wall because of the constant ringing of the loud shouts. "Shirley, Queen Shirley," Roger shook the bars screaming,

"Let me out, let me out of here!"

No one paid any attention to him. There was a metal trash can by the door of the cell. It was so heavy that it took two men to lift it. Roger, in his haste, tripped over his shoe and fell against the can, knocking himself out.

There he lay until morning. Opening his eyes, he smelled ham and eggs and heard children laughing and playing. But, there were no bars. He touched his face and then beat his chest to see if he were still alive. He was now sitting on the ground, in front of a barn. A very fair-skinned little girl he had never seen before ran up to him, crying *to Roger,*

"Daddy, Ma said breakfast is ready."

He grabbed and squeezed her arm, asking, "Daddy? Little girl, who are you?"

"Daddy, let go. You're hurting me."

The little girl broke loose and ran toward the house. Roger yelled as he chased her. She ran into the house with Roger right behind her. He slammed the door after entering, took two steps and grabbed his chest as he heard a stern voice say,

"Our next witness will be Roger Porter. Roger Porter, please take the stand," said the judge.

Chapter Five

Prison Can Be Devastating

Roger was in a courtroom loaded with people from all walks of life. A police officer walked up behind him as he approached the witness stand and a clerk came and told him to lift up his right hand.

"Do you swear to tell the truth, the whole truth, so help you God?"

As Roger was brought up never to swear, he just stared at the man. Then, Roger looked nervously around him at all the angry people.

Once again, he had no idea what he was into. Meanwhile, the attorney yelled at him,

"Did you hear me, boy?"

"Boy?" Roger assumed he must be somewhere deep in the South.

"Yes, sir," Roger said.

After being sworn in, Roger took his seat. An attorney, who was about 60 years old, with a chiseled-face and short-cropped hair, walked up to him and looked him straight in the face.

"For the last time," he asked, "did you kill Shirley Porter?"

Roger lost it. "What in the hell are you talking about? Shirley is my wife. Would I kill my own wife?"

"That's what we'd like to know," shouted the attorney, who was very upset as he accused Roger on the witness stand.

"The reason you killed Shirley Porter is because she found out that Rene was pregnant with your baby. Isn't that true?"

Shaking violently, as if he were preparing to have a nervous breakdown, Roger cried out,

"No, no! It's a set-up, it's a set-up! Rene killed her. I know she did," Roger continued as he gasped for air.

"Well, this is a different twist Mr. Porter. How do you know she killed her? Were you there?" asked Attorney Peters, with eyebrows fully raised.

"No, I was not there. She told me she did it," said Roger as he was loosening the top button on his shirt.

"Mr. Porter, do you know the penalty for perjury?"

"Yes, and it's a lot less than death."

"Roger Porter, are you trying to be smart?"

"No I'm not, but I'm not lying," retorted Roger.

The attorney looked at the judge and nodded his head. It was as though the whole scene flashed before Roger and the next words heard from the judge to the jury were,

"How do you find the defendant, Roger Porter?"

All twelve in the jury stand stood up and looked at Roger.

One little lady on the end, grasping a piece of paper, responded, "We find the defendant, Roger Porter, guilty."

Roger jumped up yelling, crying and throwing up his arms.

"You people are crazy!"

Next, the judge stood up saying, "We sentence the defendant, Roger Porter, to life in the Jackson Mississippi Penitentiary." The judge picked up the gavel and began beating the podium.

"Court dismissed!"

No sooner had the judge pronouncing sentence, then Roger, with arms stretched out as far as they could go and fingers spread farther, was yelling.

"No, no, stop, stop!"

He couldn't take the mental pressure, so he squeezed his eyes tightly and yelled again,

"Please stop!"

When he opened his eyes, Roger found himself lying on a man's lap butt-naked, in a gay bath house. The man spanking him, in the same rhythm as the judge's gavel, was Antonio. A number of men were standing in circle, watching as Roger got spanked. They were drinking, laughing and performing all sorts of sex acts.

Roger was hysterical. "This is an abomination," he yelled.

Antonio, who was twice Roger's size, began to spank him harder. Antonio had on a leather cap, large chains crisscrossing his chest and was otherwise naked. Roger lay across Antonio's lap and both of their penises touched. Roger tried to fight, but Antonio began twisting Roger's arm behind his back and forcing him to lie there.

Then, the unimaginable happened. A very tall six foot, seven inch tall rock-star-looking guy by the name of Theo appeared, carrying the largest jar of Vaseline Roger had ever seen. He asked Roger,

"Are you ready for some real pleasure?"

Roger knew that his ass was in lots of trouble now, and in more ways than one. He saw Theo go to other guys in the room and watched as they grasped a small amount of Vaseline from the jar and applied it to their own penises. Roger was hysterical. With a strong arm, Antonio held Roger down. Theo came towards Roger with some Vaseline on his fingers and began to smear it into Roger's rectum.

Roger jumped, bucked, wiggled and kicked, yelling, "Get away from me, you faggot!"

Theo held the jar up while he laughed at the top of his voice,

"When we get finished with you, we'll see who the faggot is. You poked Shirley for 15 years, and now it's time for you to get poked."

Roger yelled back, "Keep her name out of your mouth."

As Roger was yelling, a guy with an erection named Randolph, stepped out of the group and moved towards Roger. It was one of those erections that looked like it was big enough to throw over your shoulder and burp it. As he approached Roger, there was a look of terror on Roger's face. Randolph walked up to Theo, who was still holding the Vaseline jar, and stuck his hand in while staring at Roger's ass. He began to lubricate his penis up and down.

Tears were rolling down from Roger's eyes. In his mind, he was picturing a woman having a baby for the first time, but in reverse. Instead of the baby's coming out, it was going in. Roger pleaded with Randolph,

"Please don't do that to me. Please don't, I'm a virgin."

All of the guys laughed as Randolph continued looking at Roger's ass and said,

"Well, you won't be for long."

Laughter continued fearlessly. Before Roger knew it, another guy named George moved forward with a slight limp. He, too, had an erection and his target was Roger's mouth.

"Would you like an Oscar Mayer Wiener?"

Roger was so frightened that he could not catch his breath. He was feverishly praying on the inside saying, "Lord, if you are real, please help me get out of this."

George stood in front of Roger as he was forced to lie on Antonio's lap. George began to rub Roger's bald head. Then, he slowly rubbed his neck and started pulling on his ear lobes. He rubbed down the middle of his back and down to Roger's small, round butt. It was a touch unfamiliar to Roger especially coming from a man.

Roger began crying even more. It seemed his mind was twisted, as he began having a slight erection from the subtle touch George had given him. George kept rubbing. As Roger was still lying across Antonio's lap, Antonio felt Roger's erection against him. Antonio's hand crossed Roger's thigh and went underneath and grabbed Roger's penis.

"Well, what do we have here young man? Are we getting a little excited here?"

Antonio kept massaging Roger. Meanwhile, George played with Roger's ears and began to approach

Roger's mouth again.

"Don't you think bigger is better?" asked George.

Roger was *thinking* all sorts of things. He decided if George put his penis in his mouth that he would try to bite it off. On second thought, if he did that, George would surely kill him.

Peter, who appeared to weigh 350 pounds, came from a back room with some other guys and also moved toward Roger. He pulled Roger off of Antonio's lap and told Antonio to get up. He then took Roger and tied his hands and legs to the chair that Antonio had been sitting on. Roger was too scared and too weak to put up a fight. He was at the point where he was about to get violated at both ends, ass and mouth. Roger started to shake uncontrollably.

George grabbed the shaft of his penis and began to rub it across Roger's forehead, then circled it around his cheeks. George slowly slid his penis to Roger's mouth, but, Roger had his mouth closed tightly.

"You don't want us to have to force it in, do you, snarled George?

Roger knew it would make matters worse if he didn't cooperate, so, with a frown on his face, he very slowly and reluctantly opened his mouth.

"Come on boy, you can do it. You've eaten hot dogs before," said George, with a big grin on his face.

George held the back of Roger's head as, inch by inch; he was forcing his penis into Roger's mouth. Roger gagged, as though he wanted to throw up. As he squeezed his eyes closed, he heard George say,

"Open wide, I need to go deeper."

With great fear, Roger closed his eyes and opened his mouth wide. As he looked up, there he was in a dentist's chair, being prepared for an extraction. The dentist repeated, "Open just a little wider, please."

Roger waved his hand at the dentist, indicating for him to wait a minute because he needed to swallow. Then, with joy, Roger said,

"Oh, I'll open it as wide as you want," as he laughed.

By far, the bath house was the most terrifying thing Roger could have experienced.

Sitting in the dentist's chair he noticed a picture of a beautiful skyline. Roger asked the dentist where that was. The dentist looked at Roger strangely, because everyone living in New York knew that was the New York skyline. When the dentist told him where it was, Roger was very pleased. He had always wanted to go to New York, but he'd never imagined it would be this way. He had heard so much about the Broadway plays and the television shows. He even wanted to go to Coney Island, which was only about an hour and a half ride from where he was now. The dentist finished the two extractions Roger needed.

Then, Roger stood up to go to the front desk to pay, which was the automatic thing to do; but, Roger didn't have any money on him. When he went to the payment window, the assistant said,

"Mr. Porter, have a good day and we'll see you back in a month."

"A month you say?"

"Well, yes, so we can do a follow-up," said the nurse with an odd look on her face."

Roger was now curious about the cost and asked how much he needed to pay. Although he didn't have any money, he wanted to see what kind of payment plan had been worked out.

The nurse looked at him and smiled, saying,

"Oh, Mr. Porter, I meant to tell you that your wife Shirley came in and paid the bill already."

"Shirley came here?" Roger said, as his mouth dropped open. He went on to inquire, "What did she look like? What did she have on?"

The assistant slowly looked up at Roger as though something were seriously wrong; but she just smiled politely. "I'm sure you'll find out all of that when you get home."

"Get home, but I live in St. Louis."

"Yes, I know, and here's the ticket your wife left for you."

Roger could not believe this merry-go-round of a life. Then, the assistant added, "By the way, you will be able to see one of our doctors in St. Louis for your follow- up. Just call us here and we can reschedule your appointment for St. Louis. Hope you'll have a wonderful day."

Roger walked out of the dentist's office, minus two teeth, with a numb mouth and a ticket to St. Louis. As he went to the elevator, a sense of peace came over him. He pushed the button and waited patiently. When the door opened, he slowly walked in. An elegantly-dressed elevator man was inside wearing a tuxedo and white gloves. This elevator had thick, burgundy carpet on the floor, mirrored- walls and a crystal chandelier that sparkled brightly as the lights hit the prisms.

"Good afternoon, Mr. Porter," said Roscoe. "Your clothes are hanging there."

Roscoe pointed to them, letting Roger know that he needed to put them on immediately. This elevator was so large that it had a small closet in it. Without hesitation or thought, Roger grabbed the clothes and went into the closet and dressed, smelling the sweet fragrance of lavender that filled the elevator.

After he had gotten dressed, he folded the clothes he had been wearing and put them inside a beautiful Gucci suitcase that had his name engraved on the handle. Roger started to say something; but, then he thought, "No, maybe I shouldn't. I'm not going to mess this one up."

Roscoe handed him the suitcase and dusted off Roger's Yves St. Laurent suit. He looked absolutely fabulous. The elevator finally stopped on the ground level. As the doors opened and he stepped out, he found himself inside the Ritz Carlton Hotel. One could see the glitter in Roger's eyes. As Roger walked, he felt the affluence around him. Through the large, glass-door entrance, Roger saw a white stretch limousine parked in front. When the chauffeur spotted Roger coming toward the exit, he offered his right hand to Roger, welcoming him, for he had been awaiting his arrival.

In amazement, Roger got into the limousine. The chauffeur had a very pleasant personality; and, as he was driving, he asked Roger, "W-w-would you like the scenic route or take the sh-sh-short cut?" The chauffeur had a stutter.

Roger smiled and said, "The short cut to where?"

"Y-y-you, did know that you were going to meet the president, didn't you?"

"President who?"

"The p-p-president of the United States," said the chauffeur, excitedly. "The president was so honored that you donated two million dollars to the "Nurture a Child's Gift Foundation," that he will be honoring you tonight at the Annual Fundraiser here in New York City."

Roger thought maybe he was having a crazy nightmare. One minute a lady's trying to seduce him; the next minute a man was trying to stick his penis in his mouth and then the dentist is taking out his teeth. Above all, Roger didn't know he was rich. "How in the hell did this happen" he wondered, "and when did he give away two millions dollars?"

The chauffeur took a road which seemed to be very long. As they went along, the chauffeur kept looking at Roger in his rearview mirror. Roger would catch his eye and they went back and forth. The chauffeur was looking at him, because he had seen Roger before, but he didn't know where. Roger lowered his head; and, when he lifted his eyes, he noticed the chauffeur had driven in front of a beautiful castle where the fundraiser was being held. Some of the Who's Who in the world were there. Many people walked up to Roger and shook his hand, for they all knew of his enormous contribution to the Nurture a Child's Gift Foundation Fundraiser.

Roger felt very comfortable among the rich. It was as though he was meant to be there. People were thanking him so much for his contribution that they never gave him a chance to say a word, except for "Thank You." Had he been allowed to speak, he would not have known what to say. So far, everything was working in his favor. As he walked around in this beautiful castle, he noticed all of the fine furnishings.

It was really something for Roger to see, since he had never been around the wealthy and had never before been in a castle. Waiters and waitresses were continuously walking by with shrimp cocktails, drinks and other fine finger-foods. Roger, literally, thought he had died and gone to heaven.

A young woman was playing a beautiful melody on the harp. Roger was drawn to the music; and before he knew it, he was standing close to her as she played. She turned her head and smiled. He noticed some very shiny gold business cards on a little table by the harp, so he took one and put it in his pocket. He continued to listen for awhile and then eased away.

As he moved on, he passed a waiter and asked him where the restroom was located. The waiter pointed toward the east wing of the castle. Roger thanked him and headed that way. He entered an absolutely gorgeous restroom. The toilet seats, made of pure gold, sat on toilets that rested on the marble floors. The chandelier had to have cost at least a hundred thousand dollars. Roger went to the urinal and relieved himself. He then walked over to the sink, and the bathroom attendant handed him a towel with his initials, R.P. on it. Roger could not understand how this could have happened.

What he didn't know was, on the mailing list of all of the attendees, there appeared not only names but a picture, as well. It was the bathroom attendant's duty to make sure the correct person got the right towel and he had studied the names and pictures for weeks. He did a superb job of remembering which towel belonged with each guest. Roger bowed his head and thanked him and proceeded to the exit door.

When Roger went to the door and opened it, his mouth flew open as he found himself standing in a field with an auction block for slaves. Many black men were being auctioned off by slave owners and Roger was next up for bid. A man from behind grabbed him and snatched his nice suit jacket and shirt off, exposing his chest. Looking at Roger, many of the slave owners were very excited, because he seemed to be strong and healthy. These were the characteristics of a good, hard worker. Roger tried to resist and the man pushed him down and said,

"What in the hell do you think you're doing, boy?" Roger looked him in the face, but he couldn't utter a word.

Finally, Roger was up on the block. He actually thought he was losing his mind. The bidding went on and Roger was sold for two hundred and thirty dollars. He was now owned by a white sharecropper from Mississippi. He took Roger to his home without any resistance from Roger. The next day they worked and worked. This sharecropper worked another farmer's land for a share of the crop.

Roger was a very hard worker and he slept in his new owner's barn.

One day, Roger was sitting in the barn alone, when there was a knock on the door. He hopped up and peeked through one of pieces of chipped wood from which the door was made. To his surprise, it was a beautiful young girl, the farmer's daughter. When Roger saw who it was he was afraid to open the door. He then asked, "What do you want?"

"Roger, I would like to talk to you for a minute," the young lady said with a quiet voice.

"What could you possibly want with me? Do you know that if we are found talking together, I would be lynched?"

"Oh no, you won't be lynched. My Ma and Pa aren't here. They went to town and won't be home till sundown."

Roger thought about it and opened the door. The young girl came in.

"What is your name?" Roger inquired.

"My name is Rebecca, and I was home alone and wanted to talk to someone."

"But you know you shouldn't be talking to me." In the back of his mind he thought about how comical his wife Shirley was at times. When the girl said her name was Rebecca, his wife probably would have asked her was she Rebecca from Sunnybrook Farm. The girl continued,

"No one will know we've been talking, it will be our secret."

"We are really taking a chance, but I trust you for some reason," said Roger.

Rebecca sat in the corner of the barn by a tall post. She began to talk about a lot of things, but she had something very important to tell Roger.

"Roger, I would like to tell you something, but you must promise you will never tell anyone. I mean, sooner or later they *will* find out."

"Find out what?"

Rebecca lowered her eyes and said, "I'm pregnant."

"Well, what the hell do you want me to do? I'm sorry, I didn't mean to curse, but don't your folks know?" "No, they don't and I'm afraid to tell them," Rebecca confided.

"Well, what are you going to do when you start showing?"

"This is why I'm going to need your help. I will probably start showing in three months, and I need you to say you heard a ruffling sound and you saw some men run off with me."

"I do not understand you. If that's the case, why aren't you leaving now?"

"Every year, during the summer months, my aunt takes this long trip. I want to go and stay with her until the baby comes, but she's not back yet. As soon as she returns, I will leave. The only reason I'm telling you now is that, just in case I get sick, you will know." Rebecca began to weep.

Something was not clicking with Roger, although he went along with the whole idea. Then Roger asked,

"Where's the father?"

"I can't tell you that; because, if I do, someone would get killed or go to jail."

"Is it that serious?"

"It's more serious than you think."

"If you say so," said Roger with this concerned look on his face.

Rebecca remained there and talked with Roger for an hour, until they heard a horse and buggy pull up. Rebecca's parents had returned. Roger jumped up in fear, saying.

"I thought you said they weren't coming home until sundown."

"I thought so, too. What am I going to do? The only way I can get out of here is through the front door."

Roger was very nervous; and then all of a sudden, Rebecca snatched off her clothes and ran out of the barn door, screaming,

"He raped me, He raped me!"

Roger ran behind her, yelling,

"She's lying. She's lying, I never touched her!" Rebecca's father ran into the house and got his shotgun and came out shooting. Roger dropped to the ground, rolled and then he stood straight up.

He found himself standing at a firing range for the police academy. Roger dropped to his knees, muttering, "Oh, God, thank you."

All the other police officers started laughing, because Roger had finally shot a bull's eye. They had no idea why Roger was saying thank you. Many of the officers came and patted Roger on the back for his accomplishment.

The only thing Roger could do was smile with great joy in his heart, knowing he wasn't the one who was getting shot. He soon left the shooting range and thought about how he was going to get home, wherever that was.

Chapter Six

Be Careful Who Picks You Up

All of the men had left and there was not a car in the parking lot. Roger thought this was very strange, so he started walking down a nearby street. He had no idea of the direction he was going and he didn't know where he was. It was a very peaceful road and every now and then you would see a vehicle. This shooting range was about ten miles from the residential area. As he continued to walk, a car slowly pulled up beside him and the driver tooted the horn.

"Hello sir, do you need a lift?" inquired the young man who was about 20 years old.

"Yes, I do. Thanks. Where are you headed?" asked Roger.

"I'm headed for town, so can I drop you off anywhere going that direction?"

Roger thought about it for a moment, because he didn't know where he was.

"Well, just drop me off near the closest drugstore."

"That's no problem, because the closest one is in town about eight or nine miles away."

Roger felt a little secure for a moment because he felt he was getting somewhere. He and the young man had quite an extensive conversation. With the uniform Roger had on and the fact that he was coming from the firing range, the young man knew that Roger had something to do with the police force. However, the young man never asked Roger why he was walking or where his car was; and,

Roger didn't volunteer the information because he didn't know either.

Roger noticed a little cross that was glued on the dashboard and then he asked,

"Young man, are you a Christian?"

"What is that?"

"You mean you don't know what a Christian is? You have this cross on your dashboard."

The young man responded with, "Well, this used to be my Grandfather's car; and when he died, it was given to me, so I didn't question what the cross was for."

Roger thought this was very strange and decided to find another angle with which to question the young man regarding religion.

"Have you ever heard about Jesus?"

"No, I haven't. Who is he, a politician or something?" asked the young man.

"I wouldn't say that," commented Roger as he began to laugh.

"Well, who is he?"

"Actually, he was a man who died for the world, to save us."

"To save us, save us from what? There's nothing here but problems."

Roger continued, "I know, but he will comfort us and guide us when we're having problems. Just think about it. I was walking down the road and wasn't sure where I was going and you stopped and picked me up."

The young man asked, "Did Jesus make me do that?"

"I would say so," said Roger.

"How did you find out about this dude?"

Roger could not help but chuckle, because the young man actually did not have a clue who Jesus was and he was calling him a dude. Although Roger understood his language, he had never met anyone, around this young man's age, who hadn't at least heard the name Jesus.

Then Roger thought he'd ask God for wisdom and began to talk the same language as the young man.

"Well, you see this dude was the Son of this Brotha', whose name we call God."

"And who is God?"

Unbelievingly, Roger asked, "So I see, you haven't heard of God either?"

"Naw man, these dudes must have been around before my time."

"Yes, they were, and they were here before my time, as well."

"So, what's so great about them?"

With deep thought, Roger continued,

"You see, the dude, God, knew there was a problem on earth; and, the people had a hard time trying to do things right. So he sent his cool Son down to rap with them and some dudes got together and hung the brotha' on a cross, because he was so nice."

"That's some cold shit."

"Yeah, I thought so too," said Roger as he bowed his head. "Anyway, when they hung him, he died. Then, in three days, he got up with all power in his hands."

The young man replied, "Man, that's cool, shit! You sure he wasn't smoking any pot? I guess he had a three day nap. That sounds like a magic trick."

"I guess you can look at it that way, but without the pot," Roger commented.

"So what happened after that? I mean, how is it that you believe that story?"

In a serious tone, Roger said, "It's supernatural and you just have to believe in Jesus and you will be saved, too."

"Man, stop bullshitting. You're trying to figure out a way to ask me for some money to pay for it, huh?" Roger replied, "No, it's free".

Bewildered, the young man said, "I'm not getting it. When I believe in this dude that I never met, then something cool is going to happen to me?"

"Sort of, I mean, you will get this feeling that He is always there to help you."

Still not comprehending, the young man asked, "Help me do what? If that's the case, he wouldn't have let my grandfather die."

Roger explained, "He always comes back to get his children."

Children?" Hell, my grandfather's old ass was eighty and that's not a baby."

Roger was constantly laughing and then he said,

"Can I tell you a brief story of what it's like for Jesus to come and take you back?"

"This has to be a good one!" laughed the young

man.

Roger rolled down his window, letting in a little air. He knew, in his heart, that he had some explaining to do to this young man who was really green.

"Once, there was a lady who had five children in a two-story house. Every night, she would read them a story; and each one would fall to sleep. Carefully, she would pick each one up in her arms and very quietly take them upstairs and put them in their beds. Every night, she did this five times."

"So, what's the point?"

Roger continued, "The point is, this is the same way each of us returns to Jesus. For those who have accepted him, he will take us home, one by one."

"That's interesting. So what you are saying is that maybe my grandfather is with Jesus, who is the son of God. Man this is some creepy shit. OK, you can tell me the truth now. You smoke Crystal Meth, don't you?"

"No I don't. Never had it in my life but I can imagine how you feel after hearing all of this. "Do you remember when you were first learning how to drive a car and you didn't know anything about it? Someone had to teach you."

The young man hit the dashboard. "Yeah, I had a helluva time believing this damn car wasn't going off the road; but, after a while, I got it."

"That's the same way we learn about Jesus. Someone has to teach us about Him. He will give us divine revelation of what we were taught and then you will begin to want to know more. A person can only teach you so much, but the rest is divine revelation. In other words he'll teach you personally."

Now, the young man was excited. "Oh, it's that easy? So what do I need to do?"

"First thing you need to do, so you won't kill both of our asses is pull this damn car over so we can pray," shouted Roger.

"Pray? What the hell is that?"

Roger explained, "Look, just follow me, the same way you followed the person who taught you to drive." Roger grabbed the young man's hand and the young man snatched it back.

"What kind of freaky shit is this? Why you need to hold my hand?" he questioned.

"Okay, I won't hold your hand. Just bow your damn head and repeat after me. "Dear God."

"Dear God."

"I know that I am a sinner."

"A who?"

"A sinner."

"What in the hell is that?"

"It's a person that is not perfect."

"Hey, no one's perfect."

"That's the point. You are just recognizing that your sorry ass is not perfect and you need help."

"Okay, asshole," said the young kid as they both began to snicker.

Roger knew that if he didn't talk the young man's language, he would never get him to understand a few things about life. Consequently, as the young man cursed, so did Roger.

"Look, I'm not an asshole. If anything, I'm trying to keep your ass from going to Hell."

Confused, the young man continued,

"Now, you're trying to send me some place else. Where in the Hell, is Hell?"

Roger tried one more tactic. "O.K. Look, just listen to me and repeat everything I say and don't stop until we say Amen.

"Okay dude."

"By the way, I never got your name."

"*My name is Jeff.*"

"O.K. Jeff, let's try this again., Dear God"

"*Dear God*"

"I know that I'm a sinner."

"*I know that I'm a sinner.*"

"I do not know you."

"*I do not know you.*"

"Or your son, Jesus."

"*Or your son, Jesus.*" "Please help me believe" "*Please help me believe.*" "So by faith,"

"*So by faith,*"

"I believe your son died for my sins."

"*I believe your son died for my sins.*"

"And he was raised from the dead"

"And he was raised from the dead."

"Like Romans 10:9."

"Like Romans 10:9." "Hell, who is Romans?"

"Jeff, will you shut your damn mouth and repeat after me," implored Roger, as he quickly looked up

"Okay. I'm sorry, Like Romans 10:9."

"If I confess with my mouth,"

"If I confess with my mouth"

"And believe in my heart,"

"And believe my heart"

"That God has raised Jesus from the dead,"

"That God has raised Jesus from the dead,"

"I will be saved."

"I will be saved."

"And Lord"

"And Lord"

"Help my faith and my unbelief"

"Help my faith and my unbelief"

"Amen."

"Amen. And it's about time."

Roger laughed, but he knew the young man would be just fine. Then he asked, "Have you ever been baptized?"

Jeff burst out laughing, because he felt Roger was really strange. "What in the world is *baptized*?"

"It just shows that you believe. It's done by my saying a few words and you are dipped in a pool of water which shows that you believe in his burial. Your going down and my pulling you up, represents his resurrection."

Jeff asked, "Where are you getting all of this crap from?"

Roger answered his question by saying, "I have a book called the Bible. Unfortunately, I don't have one with me to show you; but, if you come across one, you should read it. There may be a lot of things you won't understand, but it will be revealed to you as you go along in life. No one who has read it knows it all. The book is almost magical."

Now Jeff was interested. "Okay, you almost have me convinced. What about this baptizing thing?"

As he said that, Jeff began driving over a bridge. Roger told him to pull over when he got to the end of the bridge, because they would be able to get out of the car and go to the edge of the river. Jeff followed instructions and Roger asked Jeff if he happened to have a change of clothes in the trunk of his car. Jeff looked at him, and asked,

"How did you know that? I never put clothes in the trunk of my car; but, for some reason, I did it today."

"Miracles happen every day." Roger smiled.

Roger and Jeff got out of the car, Jeff went and got a change of clothes and asked,

"Now, what?"

"Hold on, this is only going to take a minute. Go around to the side of the car and slip your tee shirt and shorts on."

"I can't believe I'm doing this," declared Jeff."

"Look, believe it. Get your ass around there."

Jeff started laughing. "Hey, you're pretty good at cursing too. You must have had some training."

"Yes I have, from my wife, she's a professional curser," replied Roger.

Jeff went to the side of the car, changed his clothes and came to the edge of the river where Roger was. Roger had taken off his shoes and socks and rolled up his pants legs. They both walked into the water, which came up to just above their knees. Roger told Jeff to turn around and place his arms crisscross his chest and close his eyes.

Then Jeff asked, "You're not going to drown my ass, are you?"

"No! Man, can you stay serious for just a moment?"

"I am serious. Hell, I don't even know you, and you have my ass in a river," stated Jeff.

"Okay. I'm sorry," apologized Roger.

Jeff finally turned around and crossed his arms. Roger once again explained to him that it represented the burial of Jesus Christ and that He was raised from the dead. "I'm going to baptize you in the name of the Father, Son and Holy Spirit."

"Now, who are those three dudes," asked Jeff as he dropped his arms.

"God is the Father, Jesus is the Son and the Holy Spirit is the comforter," explained Roger.

"Okay. I don't know all of these people you keep adding on but I'm going to believe you, but if anything happens to me, it's your ass."

Roger could only smile, because he understood the concern behind Jeff's warning. Roger went on to say, "But to play it safe, because there's so much controversy in the church about the baptism, I'm going to also baptize you in Jesus' name.

Confused, Jeff said, "So, in other words, there are three or four names that I have to get baptized under?"

"In reality, there is only one. My bible says, that everything you do, you do it in the name of Jesus, so I baptize that way, too. You see, Father, Son, and Holy Spirit are titles, but Jesus is a name."

"Give me an example," Jeff said.

"Okay, let me break it down for you. "Let's say, for instance, that you are a surfer."

"Okay."

Let's also say that you are a father."

"That's cool, too." Now, let say that you are also a husband," Roger continued.

"Okay, we can go for that."

"But your name is Jeff, am I right?"

"That's it," Jeff replied

"Alright. Now, I'm going to move back a little from you and I want you to follow my instructions."

"Okay, dude," Jeff said.

"Come here," said Roger

As Jeff slowly moved toward Roger, he wondered, what this meant.

Roger, sensing Jeff's question Roger said,

"Jeff, when I called you, didn't the surfer, the father and the husband come, also?"

"Yes, because all of them are in me," replied Jeff, with a little more understanding.

"That's the same way it is with Jesus. When you say Jesus' name, the Father, Son and Holy Spirit are all one."

"Oh man, that's some cool shit. Hey, let's do it!" Jeff was just smiling as he got the revelation and he turned around and crossed his arms.

Roger stood behind him, placed one hand on his back and raised the other one toward the heavens, saying, "Father God, we have here your son Jeff; and to show his new belief that your son Jesus died and you raised him from the dead, I baptize him in the name of the Father, the Son and the Holy Spirit, in Jesus' name. And so it is. Amen."

Roger held Jeff's nose and laid him back in the water and immediately brought him up. As he yelled, the first words out of Jeff's mouth were, *"Thank you, Jesus!" Right on, dude!"*

The baptism was over and Roger was filled with joy as well as Jeff. Quickly Jeff changed his clothes and got in the car. When Jeff had already taken his seat, Roger was still rolling down his pants legs as he sat on the ground, putting back on his socks. After finishing, he immediately got up and went to the car.

Once he sat down and locked his door he turned his head to the right and found himself sitting in the car with a blonde-haired prostitute, whose hair was teased about twelve inches high. There was no Jeff. Roger jumped, hopped out of the car and realized he was standing on the Las Vegas strip. He could see lights for miles and the glitter from them distracted his thoughts about Jeff, who he had previously met.

Roger was not a gambler, but he had always wanted to see some of the Las Vegas shows. He continued walking very fast down the strip. In the area in which he was walking, were a number of prostitutes. He kept walking and they were soon gone, or so he thought. He was looking in the casinos and smiling like a kid who had just received a brand-new bike.

He entered in a few casinos and saw some people laughing and jumping for joy. Others looked depressed, as though they had used the last of their savings, taken a chance on winning and lost it all.

Roger continued to walk. In his mind, he began to write a story of what may have been going on in the lives of people he passed. Who were they? How much money could they have lost or won? What were they going to do before the night was over? He was thinking of everything and he was enjoying his thoughts.

He saw a woman and her husband arguing about how they had spent their rent money just to gamble and they had lost it. Roger assumed that their landlord would not be a happy camper to hear the news, especially if he knew they had blown it in Las Vegas.

He noticed that one of the casinos was having a big magic show and he thought he would like to see it. He walked up to the window and realized that he didn't have any money. The cashier looked at him and said,

"Hello, sir. The ticket for the show is $55.00."

"$55.00" he exclaimed.

"Yes, sir, and it is our special price for the weekday shows."

"But I don't have $55.00," Roger stated.

"I know you don't. Shirley saw you walking up and knew you wanted to see the show, so she purchased a ticket for you."

Roger was stunned and asked, "Shirley, purchased my ticket?"

"Yes, Shirley Porter, she just got off duty."

"Where did she go?" asked Roger."

"I don't know, but I saw her leave in a taxi. Here's your ticket. Enjoy the show. You're just in time; it will be starting in five minutes."

Roger took the ticket and stood still for a moment. He looked at the ticket and then he looked at the cashier who only smiled. He finally went to see one of the greatest magic shows he had ever seen. After the show, he walked out of the casino and slowly walked down the street, watching all the people who were excited about being in Las Vegas.

He became thirsty, because Vegas was very warm during this time of year. He saw a little deli that had fruit drinks and he ordered a drink. The lady asked what kind he wanted and he said it didn't matter. She placed a bottle of Snapple Cranberry Juice in front of him and he backed off immediately.

The cashier looked at him. "Is something the matter? Are you alright?"

"Oh, I'm sorry. I'm alright, but can I have a bottle of grapefruit juice instead?"

"You surely can. That won't be a problem," she replied.

The cashier changed the drink and Roger grabbed the grapefruit drink and rushed out of the store. The cashier's eyes were wide open as she watched him rush through the crowd to get away without paying. This behavior was quite unusual for Roger. The cashier never bothered to call the police.

He opened the drink and the coolness of the grapefruit drink was just what he wanted. There was a trash can nearby, so he tossed the empty bottle in the can and walked on. Soon, he felt tired, saw a short bench that was sitting in front of another little deli and grabbed a seat for a while until he decided what to do. He sat so long that he had fallen to sleep. When he awakened he found himself on the third floor in a newly constructed building.

Chapter Seven

The Third Floor

The third floor was crowded as usual. Everyone was going in different directions, tending to their own business. However, on the third floor in room 302, was the usual noise and loud voice of Roger Porter. He could not stop talking and it was as though there were no end to his stories.

The nurse sat by the window and read a magazine as Roger continued to talk. On and on he went, as she tuned him out. Finally, the doctor came to his room, smiled at Roger and allowed him to continue talking. The doctor requested the nurse to excuse herself for just a few minutes while he tried to ask Roger a few personal questions. She folded her magazine and stood up to leave.

As she was going by, Roger told her that he thought the white dress she had on was beautiful. She smiled, thanked him, walked out the door and closed it behind her. In his mind, it was the first Sunday and everyone was wearing their white attire, which was always requested for communion on the first Sunday of every month. However, in this case it was the standard color of uniform for nurses and doctors that worked in the hospital.

The doctor was looking for Roger's chart and when he could not find it, he stuck his head out the door and called the nurse.

"Excuse me, Shirley; do you know where Roger's chart is?"

"Oh, I'm sorry that I didn't place it back on the door. I'll get it for you."

She went to Roger's nightstand and there was his chart. She handed it to the doctor and he said,

"Thank you Nurse Porter."

She smiled, as usual, and continued down the hallway.

As the doctor looked through the chart, Roger continued talking non-stop. He had been in this condition for more than 20 years. He was admitted to the psychiatric ward many years ago, when he had found out his wife was dating his best friend on the side. It devastated Roger and he lost his mind. His real wife's name was Bernice Porter.

He had grown fond of a nurse named Shirley Porter. She was used to his stories because many times he would put her in them. She would listen to him talk for hours, because she was his private nurse. Shirley was very comical and every now and then she would use a curse word to make her point about something and Roger would just laugh. Since he hopped from one story to another, she could never figure out what had happened in the previous one that he had told.

She heard him talk about children he never had and the time he was out on a nude beach, where he had really never been. Before Roger lost his mind, he always wanted to be a pastor. Unfortunately, since this never occurred, he just lived the whole fantasy in his head. Some days, he would talk about the large congregation he had ministered to and how they loved him. One day, he mentioned that they were going to build 100 apartment units for senior citizens. Roger certainly had a vivid imagination.

After reading through his chart, the doctor took a flashlight and examined Roger's eyes. Everything looked normal, so he told Roger that he was doing fine and he would see him tomorrow. He gently patted Roger on the back of his hand and then he left the room.

Shirley compiled all of his stories in the book you are now reading and also made herself one of the main characters.

Nurse Shirley Porter finally returned to the room and in Roger's left hand she noticed a shiny gold business card from a lady that played the harp. He had also seen this lady in his imagination at the annual fundraiser given by the president of The United States. The harpist passed by his room one day and decided to come back and play one of her instrumental tapes and offered him prayer.

Shirley looked at the card and placed it back in his hand. Roger felt a little thirsty from talking so much. At that moment she asked him if he wanted anything.

He looked at her with a slight smile on his face and said," Yes, I do. Could you bring me another glass of cranberry juice?"

END

Other Books

Self- Help : Butt Naked
(Stripping yourself butt naked dressing the real you)

How to Get Over a Past Relationship Faster than You Think

Who In The Hell is They?

Fiction: Eric, The Last Child
(For Adults Only)

Children's Book – His Eye Is On the Sparrow

Workshops: www.stewartmarshallgulley.com

STEWART MARSHALL GULLEY, best selling author has been often called The Renaissance Man because of his many professional talents. A multi-talented author. His books range from self-help to sensual mysteries all the way to children's books. An author producer, playwright are only a very few of his phenomenal talents. Constantly promoting motivational workshops that encourage people to use the gift that's embedded in their heart.

Made in the USA
San Bernardino, CA
15 July 2017